to kateln
From oma

With lots of
love

With Lots of
Love

Written and illustrated by Hans Wilhelm

First edition for the United States and Canada published in 2004
by Barron's Educational Series, Inc.

First published in Great Britain in 2004
by Buster Books, an imprint of Michael O'Mara Books Limited,
9 Lion Yard, Tremadoc Road,
London, SW4 7NQ, UK
(www.mombooks.com)

Illustrations and text © 2004 by Hans Wilhelm
(www.hanswilhelm.com)
Copyright © 2004 by Buster Books

Edited by Philippa Wingate

All inquiries should be addressed to:
Barron's Educational Series, Inc.
250 Wireless Boulevard, Hauppauge, New York 11788
(www.barronseduc.com)

Library of Congress Catalog Card No. 2003115620
International Standard Book No. 0-7641-5767-1

Printed and bound in China

9 8 7 6 5 4 3 2 1

With Lots of
Love

by Hans Wilhelm

Toby loved visiting Nana Bear.
She told great stories and made
the world's best cookies. Toby loved
Nana Bear and Nana Bear loved Toby.
Nana Bear loved someone else too:
Lottie-Dot, her yellow cockatoo.

"Why do you call her Lottie-Dot?"
asked Toby.
"Because she has lots of little red
dots on her tummy," said Nana Bear.
"Each dot is like a little red heart
and says, 'I love you'."

One cold morning, millions of little
snowflakes danced around Nana Bear's
house. Lottie-Dot felt like dancing, too.
So she squeezed through an open window,
spread her wings, and off she flew.

She didn't come back for her lunch.
She didn't come back for her snack
and she didn't come back for her dinner.

Lottie-Dot didn't come back at all.

When Nana Bear realized that Lottie-Dot
was gone, she asked all her friends to help
her search for the cockatoo.
"Oh dear. It's freezing outside," Nana Bear
kept saying. "Lottie-Dot will be so cold.
We have to find her!"

Everyone searched and searched, but they didn't find Lottie-Dot. Toby was very sad for Nana Bear.

Then, he had an idea. He made posters telling people about Nana Bear's lost cockatoo and he put them up on all the trees in the street. "That should do it," thought Toby.

LOST
LOTTIE-DOT,
a YELLOW
COCKATOO

belongs to
NANA BEAR
17 WINTER COVE

But nobody had seen Lottie-Dot.
And as the days passed, Nana Bear
grew sadder and sadder.

Toby went to her house every
day and tried to make her smile.
But it was no use. Nana Bear kept
thinking about Lottie-Dot and
every time she did, she cried.

Toby was miserable. He had never seen
Nana Bear so upset. As he walked home
through the snow, he wondered what he
could do to cheer her up.

Then, he had another idea. "I know!"
he shouted.

At home, Toby got out his crayons, paper, scissors, and glue, and drew a lovely picture of Lottie-Dot. He made Nana Bear a special card. He made it with lots of care and he made it with lots of love.

When the card was finished, Toby was very pleased with it. But just to be sure, he glued red paper hearts all around Lottie-Dot, and he signed the card with hugs and kisses.

Next, Toby asked his mother for gift-wrapping paper. But even with all the sheets of paper stuck together they were not big enough to cover Toby's card.

So, Toby found a huge sheet of newspaper and wrapped up the card. Finally, he decorated the newspaper envelope with a big red heart.

When he arrived at Nana Bear's house,
Toby found her crying. All she could
think of was Lottie-Dot lost in the snow.
So Toby gave her the envelope.

"Oh, my! How beautiful," exclaimed
Nana Bear, when she unwrapped
the newspaper and saw the card.

"I made it myself, with lots
and lots of love," said Toby.

Nana Bear hugged Toby and put the card on her mantelpiece. Then she began to fold up the newspaper it had been wrapped in.

Suddenly, Nana Bear gasped and her eyes grew larger and larger.

Paulie Road

...ter

...lgate and Co.
11 Pond Road

Harewood

Perfect for
your

FOUND
Yellow cockatoo
with red spots

Mr. and Mrs. Cottontail
...abbit Hill

M
20 w

Honey

Chalfont
Honey Bear

Finest

Fresh Fruit
Ba-Ba Sheep
3 Mount

"What's the matter?" asked Toby.

"Look, Toby," Nana Bear exclaimed, and
pointed at a message in the newspaper.
"Someone has found Lottie-Dot.
She's alive! Let's go and get her."

And out of the house they rushed. Toby
had never seen Nana Bear run before.
He could hardly keep up with her.

When they reached Mr. and Mrs. Cottontail's cottage, Toby and Nana Bear knocked on the door. After a moment, the door swung open and into Nana Bear's arms flew Lottie-Dot, squawking with delight.

"We found her sitting on our roof, shivering with cold," explained Mrs. Cottontail. "But we didn't know who she belonged to."

Nana Bear and Toby were overjoyed to have Lottie-Dot back and Lottie-Dot was overjoyed to be back.

"I know," said Nana Bear. "We must have a big party at my house to celebrate."

The Cottontails and all Nana Bear's
friends came to the party.

As everyone ate cake and drank honey tea,
Nana Bear told over and over again the
story of the beautiful card Toby had given
her and how it had brought Lottie-Dot
home. And all because it was made…

…with lots and lots and lots of love.